DUNKIN DANA

JASHIM UDDIN

Matchstick Literary
1-888-306-8885
orders@matchliterary.com

Dedicated to:-

Global Working Class People

Synopsis:- "Honey, You are not a Boss."

ONE

Hi! Good morning Dana. How are you?

Smiling sweetly Dana replies, "I am fine".

"Can I have a large coffee with almond Milk and two sugar?", Dip asked whilesmiling and shaking his head.

"Ok sir,Dana replies while leaving.

Within a minute, after making the coffee and giving it in my hand in a paper cup. Dana clicks in the cash machine Dana and says, "three dollars and fifty cents please".

Dip brings out a five dollar note from his wallet and give it to Dana. Danahanded the change says, "Thank you sir and enjoy your coffee. Have a nice day!"

"Same to you",Dip replies,

Heavy snowfall and biting cold outside. Today is a huge crowd of black and white people. Black coffee, normal coffee and Bagel of Dunkin. It'svery busy today. All wears heavy jacket, gloves and hat on the head.It's like the carnival of winter.

TWO

All are finishing their breakfast or having takeaways. The busiest train station cum sub way of New York City, Roosevelt. I am the opening customer of this coffee shop in the corner of 74 street on the top of Roosevelt. After finishing the morning breakfast from home, I have myself a cup of coffee from Dunkin. If I don't, my day will remain a mess. And likewise, my afternoon chat after office become up at Dunkin.

This station has been named after the former president of America late Franklin Roosevelt. Trains come and go every minute. Hundreds and hundreds white and black men runs in search of livelihood towards different destinations day and night. The train keeps running towards Manhattan, the heart of New York. That is why everyone says, "New York never sleeps".

Sometimes a chat happens with me and Dana in this busy 'Dunkin Coffee Shop'. Two more girl work in here. One is Bengali, named 'Pori'. And another one is an Indian girl named, 'Kajal'.

THREE

Dana is very lonely. Her child,Ovi, is too young. He is getting older day by day with the care of his only mother. Dana has invited me duringOvi's birthday. That familiar 72 street's Lion marked building the center heart of Jackson Heights.

A small birthday party. Some Bengali families with little children. The time was passing great by Dana's hospitality.

I brought a talking green colored Parrot. An artificial smart talking plastic bird that replies with "I love you'whenever you say"hello". Getting the parrot bird,Ovi was more than happy. After finishing the dinner and photo session, the cake has been cut. After saying good night to Ovi, the children left with their mothers one by one.

Then, there were only Dana and me left. Ovi has slept on the couch earlier.

Sitting on the handle of the sofa just beside and asked; do you love me?

"Should I tell the truth or just give the answer?",I replied.

Dana says, do you speak lies, do I say like that? Every men use to talk diplomatically to get the company of women especially alone and married or widowed women.

Tell me then, diplomatic or realistic, any one of them. I said, I will rather answer your question another day. Panting once Dana says, possibly that day will never come again.

I asked, why? I also will give the answer another day. She stood up from the Handel of the sofa taking Ovi on her lap to sleep at bedroom saying, Dip Bhai, its running late of the night, returned to your house, possibly Bhabi is eagerly waiting for you. At that moment the ringtone of my i-phone ringing on, the tone of the song of Rabindranath Tagore- your starts where mine ends.

Getting farewell from Dana I come out from that Lion marked building and went to Allaudin restaurant of 73 street of Jackson Heights taking a cup of tea and joined for my old chatting group- the night is getting deeper. The ringtone of the phone has rang again. I took the phone- my wife with a rough voice- what happened, won't you come home tonight? I will go to work after taking Ovi School in the morning, you will go to office.

I asked, "what's Ovi doing?"

With the same rough voice, will I be awake for you in this late night? He is still sleeping. Suddenly disconnecting the line of the phone saying, Good night.

FOUR

It is the fourth year of Ezaz's departure to the land of never returning. Dana's loneliness and without relatives in New York become tiresome. Ovi reads in Elementary School and is growing up slowly and slowly. This year in the time of summer vacation, on the leave of Ovi's School, Dana has booked Plain ticket planning with me to go to Bangladesh.

Dana is the girl of Bikrampur'sKajirPagla village and was a student of Bikrampur College once. One of the enlisted beautiful looking girls. Many memories rise in the corner of Dana's mind on the eighteen hours journey from New York. Many stories those are left by. Remembering Ezaz mostly today, I don't know why-

Seven years ago she went to America holding the hand of Khilgao Dhaka's Ezaz her husband taking D. V. visa. Two years after that comes the boy child Ovi in Dana's lap. Their family was filled with love. Dana is the daughter of Ibrahim Chairman of Dhaka's BikrampurKajirPagla Village.

One day, when Ovi was started crawling, a phone call comes from Mount Sani Hospital. It is afternoon. This is the time when Ezaz has to come back to home after finishing his work. But the phone call from the Hospital was a bad news. Ezaz having Heart attack. He is admitted in the emergency at Mount Sani Hospital.

Phone falls down from Dana's hand. Taking a Green cab and Ovi on lap she quickly runs to the Hospital. Seeing Dana, the Nurse asked removing the white cloth by which Ezaz was covered,

"Do you know him?"

Dana replied with cry, "Yes, he is my husband".

Dana grabs the coffin of Ezaz and shouting. The Nurse comes and keep Dana out. Ezaz's corps has been brought to the Funeral Home by a corps carrying Ambulance. Dana gets into the Ambulance taking Ovi with her.

The sleepiness of Dana breaks suddenly by the water of her eyes. Ovi asks, why are you crying? No dear its nothing, saying this Dana swaps her eyes. The announcement is being given then, within fifteen minutes the plain will land on Shajalal International airport. The air Hostess is requesting to everyone to tie their Sit Belts.

FIVE

At the Dhaka airport, all of Dana's family welcomes her and Ovi with flowers. American baby, Ovi has come to his father's country for the very first time. Dana fears if he will suit with the environment of this country? Fear from mosquito bites, Dana did not make the mistake of bringing all the food and water of Ovi. She has brought five luggage with her. They will stay for a month. From the airport, she goes firstat the house of Ovi's grandfather at Khilgaon. Without a father, the environment of Khilgaon becomes heavy and a weeping of water. Everyone from all beside areas came to see Ezaz's child. Ovi gets a little nervous seeing so many people.

In the afternoon, Ibrahim Chairman, Dana's father, reached the village of BikrampurKazirPagla with Dana's brother Musa taking Dana and Ovi. In the village of KazirPagla, there's also the weeping roll of the grandmother, the elder sister of Dana, the younger sister, Maya, all took Dana on the chest and the people of the village crying in tears, the people of the village and family were crying as if a crying reunion, returning to the homeland husbandless.

On this side, Ezaz's's younger brother, Awlad, means that Dina's brother in law wishes to marry Dana. Two days later, Ezaz's mother comes to KajirPagla.

Ezaz's mother, Dana's father Ibrahim chairman told, 'Brother, I have a proposal.'

Ibrahim's Chairman said, "Sister, I know what you will say." Today, 20 years of the chairmanship of what is used then? Listen Sister, your son Ezaz, my daughter's husband. May Allah bless him with heaven, my daughter is widowed as well. By the way, you are the grandmother of Ovi, and with your son Awlad, I think, my daughter does not think she will agree to the marriage. And in the same family where such a thing happened, to build a new relationship with the family again - I don't think it would be right. Don't take it otherwise.

Ezaz's mother said, 'You are a wise man, do what you feel right to do. But, take good care of my grandson and make sure he is happy. Faith to Allah. The grandson is American. Ovi will study in good schools, colleges and universities. He will be a great person and will shine face of the country in the future. Ezaz's dream must come true. You just pray to the Creator.

Ovi is your family blood child, your family will also be proud. You will see, one day, Ovi will be president of the United States. Didn't you see, the black guy Obama was the president of the United States. Obama's father was a professor at a Kenyan university, and when he married a white English woman in the United States, Obama was born. Likewise our Ovi as well will be the president of America.

Ovi's grandmother says, Mash-a-Allah! May Allah fulfills your hope? Ovi comes and get on his grandmother's lap, Ovi recognizes his Grand-mom. Dana sits on the beside seat. Giving love to Ovi, Dana says, Ovi, look she is your Grand mom. Give her a kiss. Ovi gives a big kiss to Grandmother's cheek. Ovi's Grandmother's happiness knows no bounds.

After lunch, it's time to return to Dhaka. Ezaz's mother returned to Khilgaon in Dhaka with a slightly weary mind. Told Awlad everything in detail. The dream of American of Awlad was not fulfilled.

JhantuGhotok came up with a proposal of marriage of Simon, son of Razzaq dealer in KazirPagla village. Simon is handsome-looking but three timesfails B.A., could not able to pass the test. So, he occasionally serves as manager of Razzaq dealer's fertilizer shop.

Razzaq Dealer's relationship with Ibrahim Chairman is moderate. Giving a bit positive manner to JhantuGhatak's proposal, the chairman said, "Tell Razzaq dealer to give my phone number to talk to me."

And, in the meantime arrange for a live visit to Dana and the boy to meet directly. Juntu says, "I am doing so." The next day, Jhantu arranges lunch and bride and groom visits at the Tunking Chinese Restaurant in the city of Vikrampur, with the mother of Dana and Dana's and the mother of Simon and Simon. Both liked each other. At night, the chairman's mobile phone call came. Razzaq Dealer called – 'AssalamuAlaikum, Mr. Chairman. How are you?'

Chairman: WaAlaikumWassalam. I am well. Who are you speaking?

In the reply- I am Razzaq Dealer from the North Para- I'm Razzaq Dealer, did you recognize me?

Chairman: Yes, I know that. Your elder brother Ratan Mia was a member of my log of Chairmanship.

Razzak Dealer: Yes, Mr. Chairman, you are the chairman our Union since after the liberation war. My elder son, Simon meets at your daughter with JhantuGhatak. Simon likes her.

The Chairman: My daughter also liked him. But one must say that this year Simon received a B.A. Have to pass. Don't you understand, what would it be like going America without a graduate degree?

Razzak Dealer: Anyway, I'll arrange that side. From now on, I will make Simon study at ten coaching centers. Mr. Chairman, don't worry.

The Chairman: You are talking like intelligent. Without a B. A. in the society chairs can't be found somewhere at home and abroad? You will be my Brother.

Razzak Dealer: All is wishes who lives on the up. Who knows, he has made pairs with whom?

Chairman: Listen, Razzaq dealer, tomorrow you will send JhantuGhatak to my chairman's office. I'll tell you all the things after getting it prepared. Dana will be staying in Bangladesh for two weeks.

Razzak Dealer: Okay, Mr. Chairman. AssalamuAlaikum.

Chairman: WaAlaikumWassalam.

SIX

While Ibrahim Chairman was entering his room after meeting with the councilors, getting out of the conference room finds out JhantuGhatak was eating Betel Nut wearing a Zinnah Cap on his head and an umbrella. Just after pushing the bell Chairman's peon YunusMolla comes in the room. Chairman said, "Look, Molla" Molla replies, "Yes sir" "Look, who has come to meet? Let him in."

YunusMolla knew JhuntuGhatak from before. This same Jhantu get married Mullah's brother just one year ago. He called JhuntuGhatak and appeared before the chairman. The chairman was looking at the file. Jhantu sits on a chair with a Salam. Keeping the file, the chairman said, "Will you have a tea, Jhantu?" while pressing the bell he calls Yunus and said "Give Jhuntu milk tea and give me a raw tea and bring two wraps of Betel Nut.

Molla says while getting out, "Whatever sir." Jhantu starts talking, Mr. Chairman, News are all good by the will of God? It is important to finish the work. The chairman said, "That's why I called you to my office. Have the tea first then we can start the discussion. Then the chairman's mobile rang. The chairman picks up the mobile phone, 'Mr. Member, I am in an important meeting now. Call, after an hour. I'll talk to you then. Cutting the mobile line, he himself said, "All is the plan of steeling Whet. They did not give any soil on the road, even not any peace of brick.

Oh yes, eat Jhantu Mia, have tea. Yes I'm having as well. You too. There is no one else in the chairman's room. Jhantuandthe chairman are talking while having the tea.

"You know, Dana will leave for America within next 15 days.",Chairman said.

'Mr. Chairman Sab you know next Friday is good, I know. On Friday, the good work should be finished, what do you say?JhontuGhatakasked.

The chairman said with a smile, "Jhuntu, you are very intelligent, I and the mother of Dana also thinks the same, and the next Friday will finish the good worl with a small arrangement. Jhantu stands in happiness, shakes hands with him and said, "The right thing to do at the right time." The chairman said, "Go tell the Razzaq dealer to make everything ready." Simon will fly for America as well. Jhantu says, "Mr. Chairman, I am just going to inform Razzaq dealer and ask him to make the arrangement right now" Jhantuwent out from the Chairman's office after having lunch and go to Razzaq Dealer's house, Jhantuwent straight to the door of Razzaq dealer's room where Razzaq Dealer's wife was chewing Betel Nut while half laying on the bed watching T. V.

Standing on their porch,a voice was calling him out loud, "Dealer brother .... Dealer brother........"

"What happened? Why are you screaming?",Razzak Dealer said

Jhantu enters the room. "First, arrange a sweet meal for me".

"All right", Chairman agrees. Happy to have a date for the marriage.

'Well, sit in the corner, calm down, the sweets will be coming. But tell me, is the chairman sent you with this message? Take this cold water. Yes, just the water?? Much hot today, that is why cold water, Razzaq Dealer said.

JhantuGhatak opened it all and said. Razzaq Dealer is very happy. Tells everyone on the mobile and calls Simon to come home. Simon ends his class at the coaching center and returns home.

'Listen Mr. Dealer, you have to go to Dhaka to buy gold jewelry for the wife,saysJhantuGhatak,

The dealer says, 'Everyone will go shopping in Dhaka tomorrow. There is no reason to worry about this. Razzak Dealer asks Jhantu a final question, "Did Chairman ever meet our Simon?" JhantuGhatak says with a slight smile, "Yes, how he manages his Chairmanship anyway?" Remembering Simon playing in Vikrampur College football last year. It was said to me that the boy who scored two goals for the Vrendavan College football team at Bikrampur College field last year seems to be Simon. Just understand, the chairman's eyes and head records them all and kept.

Razzaq's dealer says, "That's why Chairman just took the news with his boys and so didn't want to see Saimon personally." Jhantu says, "He keeps all the news. This is the time you go home, my nephew Selim Chowdhury will go to the mobile shop and tell you the story directly. However, it would not be right to say on mobile phones. If I give him a call, I will tell him that he have to go to Dhaka with us tomorrow. It would be nice to have a nephew with his wife at the time of purchase.

Jhantu says, "I go then. Tomorrow morning I will come." The dealer says, "Hay listen, take the rickshaw fare. Okay. Will you give it after all is done? Hey buddy, you will get it, take this. Keep this two hundred bucks, talk less. All is the will of Almighty. Stay good.

SEVEN

After completing the coaching class, Simon goes back to his father's house and did not go straight to the business office. Razzaq Dealer and Alta Bibi were watching TV half laying on bed and chewing Betel Nut.

Simon enters the room saying, 'Mother, give me rice. The rat is running in the stomach. "Alta Bibi says," You wash your face, I am giving food at the dining table." Razzak Dealer dropped the drink from his mouth and said," Simon, eat rice and listen to my two words. "Dad, I will hear, let me finish the eating first. Coaching classes in the all three coaching is a lot of trouble."

Razzak Dealer says,

"Those who reads and writes

Rides the Cart and Carriage"

That's why you must have to pass B. A. You have to sit in the big chairs in the society. If my father had passed me a B. A. then I might not have to do the dealership for the Sirs.

Alta Bibi gives Simon a meal and says, "Who are you talking to alone?" Razzaq Diller says, "No, not telling, just life real life events. Finish this and make a list of dishes for tomorrow meal.

15

The dealer says, "Listen, Alta Bibi, all the lists are on Razzak Mia's head." Even the beautiful Chowdhury house's girl like you whom I married"

Alta Bibi sits romantically next to Razzaq dealer, gently touches her cheek and says, "I know that day has changed. I will marry your boy with an American Mem. Have to buy modern jewelry." Razzak dealer says," Well, I'll buy everything as you wish. Simon comes to the Dealer's bed room after finishing the meal, and says, "Daddy tell me what is your order?" Razzaq Dealer says, "No order or wish, I heard from your mother yesterday, you liked the girl whom you met. The good news is that the father of the daughter and daughter agreed to marry you, the daughter also liked you. As soon as the girl returns to America urgently, a happy wedding day is set for next Friday."

Simon lowers his head and answers - Dad, as you wish. Razzaq Dealer says, "Listen then, tomorrow we have to go for shopping in Dhaka, weak up early tomorrow.

"Yes dad, so be it." Saying this, Simon goes to his own room. Alta Bibi was sitting beside and listening to Razzak dealer's exchanging of sentences. This time he replied, "You are saying everything like a king. The boy didn't hear anything. Listen, Alta Bibi, your son will cross seven rivers. Do you know American law? After a few years, Mom and Dad gets the America's green card." What? Alta Bibi says, "Can we go to America if Simon goes?"

Don't you see Kadar Master and his wife in North Para whom were taken to America by their son Dip for three years?

EIGHT

On this day, a wedding ceremony is held at the chairman's house in KazirPagla village. Ovi sits next to Dana with yellow colors, she's wearing yellow Saree, yellow stage around of flowers around Dana. It's a colorful ceremony. The music is playing. From the house of Simon came a flock of beautiful angel-liked girls with Rasgolla, Sundesh, Khir Mohan and twenty other type of sweets, Betel Nuts.Everyone is happy and dancing.

Preparations are underway for the ceremony of giving turmeric on the body at Simon's house. Though it is an emergency marriage, it did not stop the ceremony of a small arrangements. Ibrahim, the chairman, is a popular public servant who lives openly.

No matter what colorful dreams Dana is pursued, in her eyes, there are still some expressive memories of her marriage to Ezaz. After all, the scene of her first marriage can't be forgotten. Wandering in the mirror of her mind, life yet continues to halt like a moving train.

Wings have learned to adapt to the modern world. In American social condition she sometimes has to face tough things. The only land on which they are working to develop their talents in the right way, that is United States, which has half the world's wealth and economic cooperation in all areas of food. Dana was able to get this by heart.

Dana has decided that a partner is very much needed indeed. A Lifetime Partner with American life to celebrate life's way, will make it wealthier.

Dana has seen many Emigrant family spouses work hard and give their families and children the highest education, earned wealth, living as a first class citizen in American society. No matter how financially educated the number one family is, the American main stream society is leading the economic prosperity.

Dana chose her mate from her homeland for this decision. All the wedding arrangements are now and just waiting for the Good Friday. Arrival of greetings, best of luck to everyone. Both Dana and Ovi are delighted today. Ovi has got a guardian father.And for Dana, a husband.

Ovi's grandmother wanted to keep Ovi with her. But Simon took himself into the car and took Ovi to Razzaq dealer's house. Dana is very happy for this reason. It was as if Simon get victory over a sea of love.

NINE

Sweet night of Dana and Simon. Marriage night of spreading like petal flowers. Ovi appeared with the two on the bed as well. Ovi never slept without his mother as like the blessing of nature's grace. Deep into the night, Ovi sleeps in the chest of a bride and an ideal adolescent's mother. The first question of Dana to Simon, if I call you 'Mon' will you mind?

Just two words, my very dear, Simon says. Why are calling me formally?

Dana says with a wicked smile,"you are in my mind within the mind".

They both of them laughed verbally.

Ovi gently sleeps on one side and sitting beside the look at each other's eyes, holding her hands in his hands, eyes with eyes.

After a while Simon says, the name 'Dana' is my favorite, only wings teach us to fly. Right, but not alone, the wings will fly together with the mind (Mon). Saying this Dana hold her face to Mon's chest tightly as if she finds a safe world inside the chest of Mon.

Mild light of blue Dim Light. At the flowery marriage night, Dana lost herself in the deep corner of her mind. And once they disappeared between the one and the other, the blue screen of the glass window opened and the two woke up by the light of the sweet sunshine in the morning.

But they don't know Ovi is awake silently and looking towards Dana, he is as fortunate as any new creature of nature. Just after opening the eyes Dana sees Ovi looking at her open eyes without a blink of eyes. The red tip on the forehead. Red Mehndi in both hands, and red Benarashishe wears. Dana took Ovi on her lap and draws a red kiss on the forehead.

The first breakfast of Dana and Ovi in the early morning in her law's house. She has come with the Cereal to feed Ovi. The bride put the milk in the bowl and made the food, by the new bride Dana.

TEN

Time is running so fast. They will fly to the opening the wings to the US mainland next Thursday. There's only a memorable marriage night. This thought hurts Simon a lot in this world.

Dana says to herself - 'So, what do you think of all the time, Mon? The two are sitting on the balcony, watching the sunset in the late afternoon sun. Mon says – how? Dana says, you think after only a few days I will go back to my place of residence. And you want to pass college, coaching studies, my father's instruction to pass B. A., don't you?

Simon says, you know exactly what I thought. I will have a lot pain to live without you and Ovi. Silently touching Simon's cheeks, you foolish listener - I will go to America and submit all our marriage documents to the Immigration in just 5 to 6 months. After visa you will fly. Only one time we will talk every day. See I'm on your side.

The mind just wants the mind and only the mind...

Simon says - you have a beautiful melodious voice. Dana says this is just for the mind. Simon says, you are very romantic. How many days had passed away like this in a courtyard, Dana could not able to feel it? Dana's worry, it is the turn of returning from this KazirPagla village to travel eleven thousand miles to Far-America.

Razzak Dealer and Alta Bibi sit in the corner of the courtyard in the afternoon, having tea and chewing Betel Nut at the bottom of the Joba flower tree. Simon's younger two brothers, Emon and Mohan, came from college riding a bike.

Simon, Dana and Ovi are getting ready to return to Dana's father's house. Ibrahim chairman sends private car to Simon, Dana and to bring Ovi.

During the farewell, the two took blessing from Razzaq Dealer and Alta by reaching their feet. Razzak dealer said, 'My daughter in law, don't worry. Simon will pass the B. A. exam. My son is so happy to have you. Dana says, no father, I know Mon is very good boy. Studying carefully is not a difficult task. He will can. Alta Bibi says, mother, take good care of Ovi. Emon and Mohan will arrive at Dhaka airport tomorrow morning. I've rented a microbus. Dana says, won't you go? I will not go, but your mother will go to bid you farewell.

Go as soon as possible, your father and mother must be waiting for you eagerly. Simon says - Daddy I'm going too. Send Mom, Emon Mohan, tomorrow. We will leave for Dhaka together. God damn it, many of the neighbors gathered at the Ibrahim chairman's house. Dana has come to say goodbye. Everyone is very happy. Ovi is in his grandfather's lap. This is a great festival.

ELEVEN

The mother of Simon, brother and sister, Emon Mohan has arrived. Everyone is very happy. Only the Mon's mind is not good. Simon is sitting on the bank of the chairman's pond. Dana is about to depart from each other, and is searching for Mon. Ibrahim chairman says, the son in law is sitting in side of the pond. In the time of goodbye it should be remain upset.

Everyone does a photo session together. The chairman says, 'Simon, tighten up your mind And after a few days, you will go like this in the dream America. Only a matter of time. "Alta Bibi says, all is Allah's will, and Dana is the carrier. Brother, wish good luck to them.

Everyone got in the car. The two cars are on the way to Dhaka airport. Afternoon flight. Everyone has arrived at the airport by pushing traffic in the capital Dhaka.

Dana penetrates the Terminal-2 holding Ovi's hand. Everyone enters with a ticket. Sitting in the visitor's gallery, Dana said goodbye to everyone and left for the last tear before heading to immigration. Both eyes are wet that was facing by Mon and Dana. Both the eyes are wet. Repeatedly wiping the tears from the eyes with napkin in his hand Dana says, do not let the tears of eyes wet the way in the time of journey. Just say it and fuck. Just say I love you. "I love you too, Dana", Mon says.

Dana says, be good. Saying this Dana took Ovi disappears toward immigration. Simon just barely glances.

Looking at the path of sight.

TWELVE

Simon returns at KajirPagla with dreams, pictures, Dana and Ovi. His mind is not good. Just looking at the memorable album by turning the page on mobile. Alta Bibi loudly called Simon, "son, the night is getting late. The food is becoming cold on the table. "

"Father, eat. There is nothing to be upset about".

Just twenty hours later, the ring tone will ring on your mobile.

"Mother, I will not eat rice today. I'd like a glass of milk, said Simon.

Alat Bibi answers - Yes, I am bringing milk.

The night goes on, the dusk comes to light the light and the day ends, the time comes. On the other side,a sound of call fromMagrib and the haul from the temple. As if in the village of KazirPagla, the great gathering of sanity and peace. The Church of the village on the north side are tied with the same symphony. In Bangladesh, all religions are like cotton Fair necklace. Above all, it was a great gathering. Great meeting.

Then the ring tones on the mobile phone.

Dana on the ringing from other end, "I'm your Dana".

"Have you arrived well?Simon asks in a passionate voice.

"I just landed. Just after changing the SIM card, saying hello to you. I will call you back after I finish immigration.

Simon says, "I love you".

"I love you so much", Dana replied.

Simon yells, "Mom ... Mom Dana and Ovi arrived America well."

Alta Bibi says - Everything is God's will.

As the night getting deep, Simon gets Dana's phone call and just lost himself in the deep core of love. "Dana, your emptiness makes me cry".

"Are you sleep? Yours is now night, and my day is uphill, I and Ovi have to rest. Will talk every time either way".

"Good night my love", said Simon.

"I love you", says Dana.

THIRTEEN

The famous Landmark Lion MARKED Building is located at the corner of 8th Avenue of Jackson Heights. Bengalis live in almost every apartment. It's like a mini Bangladesh. Dana begins to live here normally. Everyone in the adjoining the flat came to see Ovi at noon. Summer in America. New York City is surrounded by green. The trees are festooned with green leaves. Everyone is happy to hear the good news from Dana. The crowd greets Dana with flowers, sweets and gifts seems a great celebration.

It's getting night, everyone is back home. Wedding video photos are showing to everyone. From tomorrow morning, classes will start at Ovi's School. Dana's work will get started. That's the favorite Dunkin Donut and the same dialogue, "Good morning, May I help you?".

In the morning, crowd of customers, coffee, donuts, bagels are having a very rush time. In the meanwhile, Deep came and appeared and says- Hello good morning, Dana.

Dana says, "May I help you?"

A customer is near to Dana, but the eyes of the Deep watches Dana, in the busiest times her and just says - a cup of coffee and the Crossest Dana says from the busy cash counter, just thank you. Please grab it from the next counter.

Deep wanted to say something but instead he just pay the $ 5 dollar bill and pick up the coffee and get out of Dunkin to Roosevelt station on the train to Manhattan. He was only thinking that is Dana forget me? Or did not say when busy - how I am?

Deep is less attentive all day long, something had happened somewhere. Dana works in the morning shift, picking up Ovi from school completing all the family activities and backs home, resting a little, and never once saying hello to Mon. Bangladesh time, it will be morning in Bangladesh waiting for that night in comparison to America. Will say good morning to Mon. So the plan of Dana to call after Ovi remain sleep finishing his homework and makes auto call. After a few ring tones then the reply comes from that end and Simon says, how are you Dana? What are you doing? Dana replies, all well. I have finished all the work. Ovi is sleeping, I have been awake to say you good morning. Have talked to you, this time I'm going to sleep.

You get up, go eat breakfast and go to class. Mon says - I am just wake up. I'll start everything after finishing talking to you.

Simon says, I have gone to bed waiting until deep night. Dana says - This way the body will get worse if you remain awake at night. I will wake you every morning in the very morning. Hearing my voice will you will think I'm your morning bird. This is why, I will be submitting all your paperwork tomorrow with 'Lawyer'. That means Green Card Visa, you understand?

Mon says, you rest a little you have no rest? America is like machine. No time to sit. Dana says, you will know when you will come, you know, this is like a living factory that makes America great. Time is short, get freshened up before breakfast. Go to class, I am going to sleep now. Will talk tomorrow. Have a beautiful day. Mon says – goodnight to you as well. Bye.

This is how the love of Dana and Mon is going on over telephone. Dana have found a new world, the waiting for immigration letter, approval will come for green card, one letter, two letters, final letter. At Mon's home address. When will be the medical tests, police clearance and all?

Then the American Embassy Dhaka Baridhara, time is not getting passed. Six months went by, the time was coming for the winter and the snow to fall. It's like a great snowfall, New York and Lucky snow fall. Eighteen inches snowfall is considered to be a good luck in America. When there is heavy snowfall that means the economy will be better that year. Luck will be good. Finally Simon gets the interview card from American embassy. In the meantime Dana send all the papers by mail. The union of Dana and Simon will happen when Simon will arrive the dream America after flying eleven hundred miles.

Simon received the visa, it is the news at 2 pm in the US. Simon calls Dana after getting out of the American Embassy. Dana was waiting for this final call. Simon took a rickshaw and came to Gulistan rides on a bus straight to Gulistan, then to Bikrampur bus, to KazirPagla. Razzaq Dealer, Alta Bibi was ready with a packet of sweets. It was a great moment. After receiving the news, Emon and Mohan from College, took the bike appeared quickly. Everyone is very happy. Razzaq dealer happily returned home after closing the shop. This time, Montu nephew DV visa is not needed. Arrangements will be made to fly Razzaq Dealer and Alta Bibi by Simon to America. It sits in his mind silently.

Simon's father in law means Dana's father Ibrahim chairman gives the good news about obtaining a visa over mobile phone. Ibrahim Chairman says with happiness, "Father Simon, will you come to our house tomorrow, we will eat together, and your mother-in-law does not see you in a long time." Simon says, "Abbajan I will come."

It is the morning in New York. Simon combines the New York time zone with the clock. Deep night in Dhaka. After calling Dana she says, 'congratulations to you.' Simon says- thank you. Dana says, two good news for you today.

Mon says, I know I will come to be your partner of happiness. Dana says another is the result of your B. A. exams come out online today. I checked and found that you have got second class passed. Oh! I had forgotten the result of my exam today. Anyway, thank you very much. I've been able to keep your father's word.

Dana says. I'll be fresh. I will go to work after dropping Ovi at school, you sleep. Tomorrow I will inform all the plans at noon time of Bangladeshi time. Good night and good sleep honey. I love you so much. Dana says- thanks.

FOURTEEN

Morning rush hour at Dana's Coffee shop 'Dunkin Donate', everyone is busy.

At the same time, the arrival of Deep at the same speed, the same smile, "Good morning Dana, how are you?"

"I'm fine", said Dana.

"Black large size coffee with Almond Milk and Sugar".

Dana go to the cash registers are served coffee at the delivery counter and saidthank you. In the crowd of many customers, Deep says in Bengali,"If you are free at Noon, call me".

 Dana did not say anything yes or no. This busiest time with customers. Deep with a little amnesiagoes to the subway.

Dana finished working for five hours and picks up Ovi from the Babysitter and goes home.

Dana just thinks how she will inform Deepak about her wedding? She makes plan, one day, will report the news with dinner throwing a party. Next Sunday, Dana will also be on a holiday as well as Deep.

One day, at noon Dana gives a phone call. Deep was much happy having the call.

"Will you have dinner at my house next Sunday?"

"Anything special? Birthday or anything else? Deep asked.

Dana did not say, there are no such occasions. It has been many days, there is no such thing. "It's been a long time since I came from Bangladesh. We don't have to talk so much for long............"

"I will come to the place", says Deep.

FIFTEEN

At around 7 pm, Deep pressed the bell on the Lion Marked apartment at the corner of 72 Street.

Dana asks from the inside,"who is this?".

"It's me, Deep".

Dana opens the Bell and unleashes Gate's auto switch. When the door comes to the 4 / D flat on the 4th floor with the elevator, Dana opens and the door and let Deep take a sit.

Deep says with a thoughtful mind, "How are you?"

" Black Coffee or Almond Coffee?", Dana replied.

"Whatever you like?"

Dana says, "Yes."

Sitting in one corner of the living room sofa, making coffee she says, 'Have a sip on the coffee, Deep, it is ready to Drink." Dana undoubtedly says that the event and the mind of the wedding took place in Bangladesh. Mon will arrive in New York on March 7th.

Deep just says, 'Congrats!"

"Thanks!".

All the words of Deep remain stopped.

Dana says good night.

Deep replied, "Bye".

SIXTEEN

Dana gives a call to Mon at New York time. She totally explained how the plane will come to New York. Simon will be booking tickets in the first week of March, the last of the winter. Dhaka to Dubai to New York. John F. Kennedy International Airport.

As per Dana's advice, Simon's tickets and shopping luggage all are ready. Looking forward to that sweet day. When will he get Dana? It's a long wait. Every day they talked. The especial moment for him, when he will cross the seven seas and thirteen rivers and will fly across the Atlantic to meet her.

At J. F. K. Airport, Dana is standing at the Arrival Receiving Hall. Finishing the immigration Mon takes the luggage trolley and finds Dana standing out there. Two people wearing jeans and jacket, red roses are in both Dana and Mon.

Two people hugged each other.

Mon kissedOvi on the forehead. Then comes a cab, and they go to the apartment at Lion Marked building in Jackson Heights.

SEVENTEEN

Just a thirty-minute drive from J. F. Airport. The cab is moving forward, with the scenic view from the fast-moving cars on the American Highway Simon feels that a new world is embracing him.

Dana was pointing and showing the locals next to the rally. Simon just observed and said,"One of the truly wonderful world Americais, I am really lucky".

After arriving Dana's home, Simon ended up exhausted and get asleep very soon having the lunch. At the afternoon, Dana, Ovi and Simon go out and make a trip to the Bengali prone area called Jackson Heights. Simon says to Dana, 'It seemed like a shopping area in Dhaka, all the familiar faces, everyone sitting in the Abdullah Sweets, had a few of the white Roshogolla. Simon's favorite Roshogolla, he couldn't imagine how it has come to America. When the dusk rolls around, you will now be taken to the well-known Manhattan light-shining Time Square. The three enters the subway. Dana shows Simon how to cut an e-ticket for the train, and Simon carefully learns how to cut a ticket from the machine.

Riding on the E-train from 42 Street 8th venue station, and after getting down they become walking at 7th Avenue 42 Street of

Time Square area. The two started the photo session by their I-phone. And Ovi took picture on his I pod.

It is about ten o'clock at the night. This is a pleasure, everyone is hungry then including Ovi. Everyone sits on Beef Burgers and drinks at Macdonald in Time Square.

Macdonald Restaurant is Ovi's favorite food place to eat. They had a lot of fun watching photos in different poses. Ovi is busy too. Ovi is very happy watching thousands of people come and goas well as the shining lights of Time Square.

It's time to leave the Manhattan Times Square and return home.

"I will not go by train now, let's go home with a Cab", Dan said.

"Let's go back by train though, it feels good in the underground subway though it is hundred years old. Still the modern train Subway", said Simon.

"Mon, it is just the beginning, you will ride buses as well as trains. Take the experience of riding a cab today".

"Why? I did the first American Journey by Cab from the Airport.Have you forgot that?", Simon asked.

It is his first time to Jackson Heights from Manhattan. Simon asks how much is the fare of thecab. Dana says it's seventeen to twenty dollars and depends on the traffic.

"Even traffic jams this night?", he asked.

"Hey dude, the New York Never sleeps. Throughout the night the traffic was moving", Dana answered.

'Mummy let's ride a horse then, Ovi requested.

"Not today, Sunday will be your school holiday, you ride then", Dana said.

Dana hails the taxi. Ovi does the same. They all got into the cab and told the address to the driver. The cab is running, crossing the Queens Bridge to the Northern Bluebird at Jackson Heights and to the 32nd Street Lion Marked Building. Dana paid the taxi fare by her credit card after getting down.

Simon learned how to rent a taxi on a credit card.

Dana says, "Ovi, will you eat something?"

Mon says, "You see, like my mother, ask me to drink a glass of hot milk at night."

Dana says, I know you won't sleep all night. Because of all the reversal in Bangladeshi time.It's daytime in US and nighttime there. So, sometimes it will take time to adjust.

" Oh yes, I have to call Mom", Simon says.

"Get freshen up first, drink the milk and then talk on the phone", Dana ordered.

"You get Ovi to sleep?"

"I will tell me poems, songs and make him fall asleep. I have made a good habit. I will make him listen songs, poems and he will fall asleep," Dana answered.

Dana is doing all things ready. After freshen up, Simon is sitting in the living room and pressing the TV remote button but could not find any Bangladeshi channel. Then Dana came and sat next to him saying that I have kept one Bangla Channel for Ovi's Bengali learning.

Mon says, "You should do a good job, otherwise the boy will forget Bangla".

"See?', Dana pressed remote and finds the channel.

"Click channel no. 13 and you can see Bangla channel".

Then, there was noon news in Bangladesh. Simon suddenly turned towards his motherland, keeping an eye on the TV screen for some time.

Dana said, "Give me your mind, and forget about the country." They started planning for the future. Mon is anxiously looking at Dana. Dana says, "Return your heart where thy body is."

He then hugs Dana and says, "Yes Dana, I will plan on you and Ovi." Create a beautiful world, 4,000 miles away I will create a nest of happiness. You will be the queen".

They embrace each other and lay down on the Couch and the call to Bangladesh never happens.

It was morning, when Dana opens her eyes, she saw the morning sun falling on the window. Dana pushes Simon down and says, "Get up here, we were asleep on the sofa."

"After having the morning breakfast and let's drop Ovi to school and I'll go to work. You come home and give you a long sleep and talk to the country people on the phone".

Simon says, "Good idea." Let's get ready soon.

"I make Ovi ready, you go to the bathroom and come freshening up."

"We have only one bathroom, it's not Bangladesh that will have two or three bathrooms."

Ovi enters the school gate and it is time for the two to go different direction. Dana says, "I went to Dunkin ', you go home, don't go the wrong way again, and walk straight on the 5th Avenue to the Lion Marked building at 12th Street."

Mon said," I am not such stupid that will forget the way. It is easy to recognize New York streets; all the avenue and Streets are very scientifically and mathematically made".

"Bye. Walk straight, do not be too smart now. This is America," Dana replied.

"Do not try to be an artificial intelligence".

Dana says, "I am not a robot. Bye then. Go."

Two are going in two directions, Mon is looking back at Dana again and again. Once Dana disappear, Mon goes towards the Lion marked Building. Simon rushes into the house and calls Razzaq dealer and mother. Talking about the story of America, the story of the Times Square. The mother says, "Father Simon, our wife loves you?" Mon says, "Mommy, she loves me a lot, like Ovi. Mom, green card will come after some days and then I can work. "

Alta Bibi says, "This is good news, but keep an eye on your health."

Mon replies, "Don't worry, just take care of my father." And listen, Emon and Mahon, do not let them get involved in politics beside college classes. Studying first, then comes another job."

"Son, you passed B. A. by three times, this student politics wasted your three years."

"Mom, now I understand that studying is a student's core asset. My B.A. certificate also gives honors in America, where a college degree is a great honor here. Mom, I'll sleep now and have to bring Ovi from school at 5 o'clock."

"Okay, Dad, sleep, eat rice. Ok, mother. Be well"

Simon adjust the Alarm Clock at 2:00 and gets asleep. When the alarm clock rang at 2:00 pm, Simon woke up and ran to school ready to pick up Ovi. He lined up and queue of parents. Guardian, White, Black, and Asian. Itwas like a Meeting Fair.

There is no discrimination in one school of all castes and religions. Mon just looking at those.This great country has equal rights for all. In the meantime, carrying the shoulder bag,Ovi comes in line and raises his hand and says," Dad, I am here". Mon becomes impatient, hugging Ovi and took him on lap and on his shoulders.

They go home and he says, "Ovi, you are really genius."

Ovi says,"thanks!". He asks suddenly, "Where is Mom?"

Simon says, "She is at work now."

"When she will come?" askedOvi.

Simon says, "Soon."

The two of them return home and cook Simon's food from the fridge and heat it in the microwave, "You eat, your chicken Polao."

Smiling,Ovi says, 'Thanks Dad'

It was then that doorbell of the house rang. Sitting on the sofa watching TV, Simon reaches the phone

From the other end, Dana says, "Have you warmed the food for Ovi?"

"Is Ovi eating".

" Give the orange juice in glass", she says.

Mon says, "Okay".

Dana says, "I am busy now, bye then."

From the dining table Ovi says, Dad, who call you?"

"Your Mom.",Mon says.

Can I talk to Mamoni?

"She is busy now. Talk later. Ok. I am busy too".

"I am done Daddy".

Mon says," Orange juice?"

Ovi say," No,thanks".

Simon says, "ok after a few minutes then".

Ovi says,"I am playing new game in my Ipod, don't bother me.

Simon says, "Okay, father."

Suddenly the tone of the doorbell came from downstairs.

Ovi says, "Dad, somebody call in door bell." Pressing the switch Simon talks by the Talkbutton, "Who is this?" Answer comes from the down, 'Mail Delivery Man. Please the door.' Simon opens the door and press the open button.

The Mail Man says, "Are you Simon?"

"Yes.", Simon replied.

"Please sign and receive this letter."

Simon took the yellow Mail by signing.

This is green card that hemostly wanted. Immediately, he made phone call to Dana saying, "Open your letter and see that your green card has arrived. When you return home, you will open this yellow Mail by your own hand".

"Okay', Dana said with happiness.

By saying this, Dana cut off the line. After 4 hours, she returned home and told Mon, "Congratulations." Dana says, "I'm a little freshen up and then the yellow Mail can be opened. Mon says, 'Oh, you freshen up then. Drink some cold Cranberry juice". Mon pours a glass of juice from the refrigerator, standing for eight hours Dana now feels like paradise and a littlerelaxed. Then enter the bathroom. Dana says, 'There is no time for relaxation. I'll cook for you again.

Mon says, "I'll help you then."

Dana replied, "Well done, you'll learn the cooking." "It will."

The desired yellow Mail will be opened now. Dana freshen up and comes to the drawing room. Simon takes the yellow envelope off the table and handed it over to Dana. Dana opens the green plastic card with Simon's hand and says, "This is the beginning of the life you're dreaming."

Mon says, "Thank you so much Dana."

Sitting beside Ovi says, "Can I see the Green card?

"Of course,", Mon replied.

"Bythis green card now you can apply for job legally. Oh yes, for the security card will go to the security office at Woodside. I am taking a leave tomorrow by giving a phone call now", said Dana.

 Mon asks," If not for a while, isn't it be okay?"

'Without it you will not get your salary.'- Dana says.

Mon says, "Now I understand how important it is!"

Mon says, "you get ready; I am coming after I finished cooking."

Dana says, "Ovi, go to your table and do your homework. Ovi is busy with gaming in his ipod.

"Mommy please just five minutes only".

"Okay, but not more than five minutes then".

EIGHTEEN

After two weeks, Simon's Social Security card comes by the mail. Stat ID has been completed. Dana lying in the bedroom at night."Mon, I got special news for you. Tomorrow, I will confirm your job at Dunkin at Penn Station in Manhattan. Our Area Manager, John confirmed your job. However, the training will last for two weeks. Of course, the salary will be $ 14 an hour.

"Thanks, the solution to our problem today is to sitaround idly".

Dana says, "You are so lucky, many people come to New America for three to four months just to understand the raft and the atmosphere." Simon says, "You are so smart. So, all are getting pretty quick." Dana says," I will buy a house in the next five years by saving salary from two jobs. Mon says, "Awesome plan. We will deposit one salary and spend the other." Dana says, "Smart plan."

Mon says, "Explain me a little about the map of how I would go to the subway in the morning." Dana says, "Open your phone. Now go to Google search and click on the search and write 'NYC Transit Subway', all right. Then all the information will come. If you get on the F train from Roosevelt station it will make you notice to the Peen station. And will take you to the Dunkin coffee shop. Three Bengali girls will come in and tell them your name. They have a message. The name of the store manager is Porimoni. She also speaks Bengali, Bengali. So, no problem. Now, just take asleep. Tomorrow will be the beginning of your new life."

Holding Dana in his embrace, Simon says, "What do you mean by working day?" Dana says, we are the working life means the working class. Mon says,"I understand, it's a deep thing." America is a country of capitalism."

"Intellectually and physically working people now runs the earth."

Mon says, "I understand everything." Dana removes Mon from her chest, "No need to do mischief. I'm turning the light off to sleep, fall asleep."

Mon wanders in the dream state, wandering in Dana's embrace, KazirPagla village tries to wake up again, but does not let him sleep. He comes quietly to the living room and speaks on the phone to their country, so Dana will not feel disturbed.

After the talk, Mon goes to sleep again in the bed room. He sleeps at last after doing this side and that side. You have to get up at five in the morning, set the alarm according to this.

Simon's American humble life begins today. Riding on the subway, he enters the coffee shop, arrives at dunkin and says in the cash counter in Bangla, "Are you Simon?" after saying good morning. Simon says, "Yes, I'm Simon. John emailed your infos yesterday and via email. She shows entrance door, "You come in." Simon enters, and Porimoni explains everything to him and hands a T-shirt to Simon, "Go to the change room and change it." Simon says, "Where's the change room?" "In the basement, go straight down the stairs to the right and get a closet," says Porimoni. Simon changed the dress and watches Porimoni at the refinement stand in the coffee shop.

This is how to do Coffee Making, Bagel Making, another item, Ice Coffee, Café Chinu. Total Bar Coffee items. Simon learned them in just two weeks.

Simon returned home in the afternoon. Dana did not return yet. Today, Bhabi, the next to the flat picks up Ovi from school. Her son Jimi also is his classmate.

The first question of Dana to get into the house is, "Mon, how do you feel about American working life?"

"Very simple, but has to stand eight hours".

"Honey, You are not a Boss, but you will adapt soon, everything will be fine", Dana said.

THE END

www.ingramcontent.com/pod-product-compliance
Lightning Source LLC
Chambersburg PA
CBHW020348110726
47898CB00003B/1094